Once Upon A Time

Once Upon A Time

Formulated and Written by

William Desmond Kiara

Edited by Anonymous

Edited by Anonymous

Library of Congress Control Number: 2012902833
ISBN: Hardcover   978-1-4691-6795-4
                 Softcover   978-1-4653-8875-9
                 E-book   978-1-4691-6796-1

This is a work of fiction. Names, characters, places and incidents either are the product of the author's imagination or are used fictitiously, and any resemblance to any actual persons, living or dead, events, or locales is entirely coincidental.

This book was printed in the United States of America.

To order additional copies of this book, contact:
Xlibris Corporation
1-888-795-4274
www.Xlibris.com
Orders@Xlibris.com
105261

This tale is dedicated to the

Wonderful

No matter
who you are or where you are.

Look at the spaces in this tale the same way you

Listen to the silences in music.

Tick

Tock

TICK

1

Once upon a time there was a little boy. His name was William Desmond Kerr. His father's name was William James Kerr. The boy was ten and his father thirty-six. His father was a very handsome man from Ireland. He was about five feet ten but everyone thought he was over six feet tall, as he had such an imposing air about him. He carried himself in a way that made some people afraid of him. He stretched the meaning of the word imposing.

2

The actual time was the early spring of nineteen forty, about two years before America entered the Second World War. The late Model T Fords were still on the road. They were not called antiques then, just old cars. Many of these treasures from this part of the country would make a stop at the "New World Auto Salvage Yard," located somewhere in northern New Jersey on their way to Detroit, their birth place, to be devastated.

Mr. Kerr drove one.

TOCK

3

William James Kerr's old Model T, a real Tin Lizzie, was restored. New windshield wipers, a complete oil change, radiator water topped off and a coat of cheap no-rust black enamel paint. This cheap paint had been applied by first time auto painters, his unknowing and favored two daughters.

Like its owner, it looked good from a distance.

4

William Desmond's cousin, Aunt Linnie's oldest daughter, a beautiful nineteen year old beauty, was down stairs in the living room. The flowers there were now located on the side of the room next to the windows. They could not be seen, as it was the middle of the night. The lights were out.

Her name was Leonora, but everyone called her Lily, just as they called the boy William, Billy. Billy it was, and Billy it would remain. William James was called Bill.

TICK 5

The two story colonial Manchester Connecticut house, with its blooming side yard, located on South Main Street, was crowded with all the people coming up from New York City, including Billy's whole family. There were five in his family.

Aunt Carrie, the sixty year old tightly permed grey haired woman, had mammary glands that went down to and did battle with her knees. She had gravely painful arthritic knarled hands and feet.

6

Yet with her rolled up breasts, content in their brassiere resting place, with "such a pretty face", and with her prissy tea-totaling ways, she was attractive.

I do not know how she managed to get everyone a place to sleep. There were not that many beds in her and Uncle Bob McConnell's house. She was the boss of her family of four. Uncle Bob, sixty-three, did not mind or seemed not to. He was busy with his job, his beer drinking, his baking and his betting on the horses that ran in the small neighboring Rhode Island race track.

TOCK

7

Aunt Carrie had people sleeping here, there and everywhere. That is how it to be came that the son and father were in the same bed.

8

Bill did not like Billy, his youngest child. Billy was too fragile. Bill wanted to have a strong little man with a crew-cut as his son.
That is the kind of son he should have had; a fighter, a little street wise guy, wise beyond his years, a self-protector.

9

Bill was all man. I guess that is why some people were afraid of him and why he did not want any part of Billy.

It is hard to believe, with both in the same family that Bill did not know anything about his offspring, except that he did not like him. In fact, he was ashamed of him. Ashamed that Billy would tarnish his image, an image that only an Irish man would treasure.

10

What could be better than giving the impression of being taller than you are, appearing husky and also being Irish? Without a word, he seemed to shout out, "Look at my rugged body, see my dark Irish eyes, hear my Emerald Isle brogue."

Anyone could be Bill's devoted friend and the recipient of his boastful generosity. There were restrictions though. You could be neither his wife nor his son or for that matter his brother.

That breed of paternal stinginess bankrupted Billy's money brain. Billy was never able to be friends with real prosperity.

11

TICK 12

There were also five in Lillie's family, if you did not count, Uncle **GEORGE HOGAN,** fifty-three.

A closed eyed, golden voiced singer of Irish melodies and an in bed reader of Dickens, Aunt Linnie, fifty, threw him out of the house the year before last because he drank too much. So much so that he ended up as one of those bums you would see on the Bowery.

13

That was when the Bowery was the Bowery and a bum was a bum. This bum, **GEORGE,** too afraid to get a job, destitute, deceitful, god forsaken, alley masturbator, all liquored-up and soiled, died in the shadow of the riveted iron structure that supported the elevated rails of the Third Avenue "El" train.

14

The smelly carcass, found sitting upright, its arms around a much peed on fire hydrant, seeking to embrace the passion of youth, its socks around its ankles. Its swollen bruised shoeless left foot submerged in the anointing gutter water. Its right foot just lay there. It had nothing to say.

15

It's mouth closed, sealing forever any chance of decency. It's chin up, it's eyes wide open staring at the exact moment it died, looking for the essence that took flight making it lighter in death than it was in life, when "he" became **"IT."**

16

Confirmed indeed to be a stiff, the two policemen watched for breath rather touch for pulse. **BUM GEORGE** was hauled off to the city morgue, and was identified by his disloyal, gratified oldest son. Destined soon for *sainthood,* this good for nothing was disposed of in Potters Field on Harts Island, plot H-828.

17

Her arms flailing, wailing Aunt Linnie, in spite of her lauded tones and her love of Dickens, she herself would die

18

a drunk.

When Lily's family came up from New York, she did not travel with them.

They came by train.

Those sisters of this Irish clan who did not live in Manchester lived in New York City. They congregated around 138th Street and Willis Avenue in the Bronx, an Italian-Irish neighborhood with just a few Jews thrown in to make it interesting. Because they lived in apartments and not in houses is why those same sisters had to come up to Connecticut. 138th Street was a wide cross street, running East to West. Willis Avenue was also a wide street. It ran from South East to North.

I told you it was the middle of the night. The lights were out in the entire house and the house silence matched the house darkness.

Everyone was asleep except for William James Kerr. He was awake and lying near his only, very tired, son.

Billy's head rested deep on a down pillow. His hair was slightly red, to the delight of his forty-seven year old mother.

22

The unknowing, hard of hearing, never having had a best friend, Florence, whom some people called Flo, and others Florrie, concealed her good looks with bobbed hair, front buttoned cotton house dresses and a housewife's fatigue.

It was only after menopause that she discovered that little bit of makeup, styled her hair and wore garments that allowed her beautiful self to be seen. But that was all too late.

Florrie did not have a confirmation name because she was brought up after her

recently widowed mother left the Catholic Church.

At that time a Parish priest, who knew more than God, insisted that her MOTHER surrender the three youngest of HER children to a Catholic Orphanage. Rather than do that, SHE unstrung HER rosary beads.

24

In those early days in Ireland, Bridget bravely supported Herself and Her seven children by working as a licensed nurse-midwife, a sometime abortion provider and a decider of viability.

All three were part of HER job, but she got paid for only one.

Some who knew said the deciding made HER a mean hard woman.

25

SHE had many grandchildren but had a special connection to only one. SHE was sweet and kind to Billy and he loved HER. SHE celebrated his every tooth lost.

26

BRIDGET, every-one now called HER GRANDMA, had just a few months before suffered injuries from an accident she had while crossing 138th Street. She was hand in hand with two of HER daughters. All three had been drinking. Their drinking had nothing to do with the accident.

27

It was GRANDMA'S ankle length, late 1800's, smartly fashioned emerald green coat, the bottom of which flew to and got caught up in the chrome bumper of a speeding taxi.

28

She was ripped away from those holding hands and dragged a full block on the trolley railed, cobble-stoned road, before, the too young, too eager, too fast, devastated driver knew there was anything wrong.

TOCK 29

After being in the city run Lincoln Hospital for many weeks where SHE developed severe bedsores, SHE was taken up to Aunt Carrie's house by ambulance to be better cared for. Even with the better care she did not make it, SHE was eighty two years old.

30

Florrie's too much loved, too much controlled darling, her mate replacement, her treasure, her conscripted companion had eyes that were startling blue. At his age any hair Billy had on his body was confined to his head and that hair was just long enough and wavy enough to make him look angelic. He was in an innocent sleep, the kind that belongs only to children.

31

I do not know and no one will ever know, what caused this soccer player, son of an Irish mother (who was more devout than the Italian sister of the Pope), hater of the church, and father of three to put his hand on the smooth pale flesh that covered his loathed son's right pelvis bone.

33

Moments passed. The soon to be criminal hand stayed there as the guileless boy remained in his elegant sleep.

34

This slumbering innocent prince knew all about how a father would withhold love. His loneliness, his many hurts, his humiliations, the stinginess and the just plain meanness would testify to this, but he knew nothing about how a father would give love.

TOCK 35

Now that narcissistic, callous hand moved slowly to the right, stopping at the small circular creases of flesh that revealed the geography of the boy's body. Again the perfectly proportioned, never to be punished hand rested for some time. Still no response from the ever-trusting lad.

36

After anxiously loitering for what seemed to be an incredible amount of time, that stingy hand moved down to a place that should have been the domain of Billy's future young bride. The salacious hand arrived at its target.

38

It was a tender sly touch but it was enough to cause a startled awakening. What was going on? What was causing this first time closeness? This turning, this face to face, this body to body, this hugging, this kissing, this feeling up?

39

What a time to need to have to go to the bathroom, what a time to need to pee.

Getting out of the bed in hurry and dashing to the one bathroom there was in the house, only to discover that once there, he did not have to pee after all. He did not know what was going on down there, but a little disappointed he knew he did not have to pee.

40

As the joyous Billy was rushing
back to the bed made profane
that night, he repeated to himself
many times; He does love me, he
does love me. He was so excited
that he may have said one of those,
"He does love me's" out loud.
Then came the slow, "Papa does
love me."

He could not get back fast
enough, to be held, to

be caressed, to be kissed, to get
more of that

love

TICK **42**

The way back to the odious bed took Billy to the head of the oak stairs leading to the darkened living room.

At that moment and in that place and with all his rushing, a thought did occur to Billy that caused him to hesitate, to actually stop, to stand still, to ponder,
"What is going on with Papa and me is really strange."

44

What with Lily down stairs,

Lying in her coffin.

46

Oh! Forget that, Billy was on his way to get more of that

47

love.

48

TICK **49**

Little did the poor child know that night and what followed would cause him to lead a life any fair minded judge could only deem ruined.

That night was not the night Billy found love but was the beginning of Billy's insanity. Not physical or chemical insanity but a kind of behavioral-learned insanity. The kind that is internal, unspoken, unseen, torturing only the recipient, passed down from generation to generation, getting more severe with each passing until there is no more passing.

51

In his insanity, dreams
would become nightmares,
caresses-restraint, trust-fear,
fear-terror, innocence-guilt,
pride-shame, love-loathing,
and
the joy of living-fear of dying.

52

That learned insanity would steal from him, his self, his prosperity, his sexuality, his bride, his friendships, his work, his creativity, his children and his ability to cope with all things important. But most of all, this being half dead, his craziness would cause Billy to lose his memories of the future.

It caused Billy's time on this earth to stand still, to be stuck, to be fixed, to be changeless, never to move, to be ten always. It caused him not once to be the brave unafraid, fear free adult male the universe intended him to be.

TICK **54**

No one strived harder in all things than this child-man, but just as the crown of success was about to be placed on his head, it would stagger mysteriously into the static timeless, waveless sea of unlovability and slowly sink to the bottom, seeking the familiar comfort of despair.

There was always the fear that Billy, brought up to be beholden to and brutalized by bullies, would find the pretense of living too much to bear and would eventually succumb to the siren call of

The Bowery.

Maturation is always the winner in the physical realm, insisting on growth and aging. No one is exempt, but in the psychic realm, maturation can be thwarted and childhood can persist.

Remaining ten, being a child in adult form, in the company of actual adults, is a cause for intense bewilderment, confusion and fear.

57

The fates did not look kindly on this child who was a child past childhood. They demanded of him to be a lover of women, get married, buy a house, assume a mortgage, buy a car, have a career, sign a contract, sire a child, challenge a self-confident adolescent, all of which he could not do. Although his eyes could see these things, his damaged child brain was irrevocably blind to them.

58

No, that is not right, poor Billy's eyes could not see these things. All was invisible to him. He did not see the bloom of youth, couples holding hands, mothers carrying babies, children playing, fathers laughing with their kids.

These things were unseen. Life affirming actions were imperceptible, not of his planet.

The uncaring Fates did not know that this kind of child knows only fear, withdrawal, paralysis and a loneliness that can only be described as profound. Is our sweet smelling angelic innocent prince with his slightly red hair, lost forever?

60

Dear Reader—You decide,

** or * or ***.

Not now but later.

TICK **61**

The crass fates, too quick to crucify, are not aware of the mysteries of the brain, the fragility of life and the complexity of time. They are not acquainted with what transpires when living is mutated into existing then into surviving.

62

When a dear friend becomes an imagined deviate enemy. When a dream becomes a crying out nightmare. When anxiety defines. When learning is traded for escaping from monsters. When love is lost in the blur of dread. When failure is a plea for help. When terror is one's only companion. When the thought of success is only rewarded with the thoughts of death. When withholding monetary reward is used as a means to destroy self-worth. When the stop time lasts longer than the time of:

TOCK **63**

Once Upon A Time

Throughout it all, even though his time was halted, Billy and the Fates knew that if you were Irish, fun will be fun, a song will be sung, and a dance will be danced.

TICK **65**

Now the time is the spring of 2010 when America is in two questionable and disastrous wars and when new hybrid Fords are first on the road. Long dead, Mr. Kerr did not own one.

66

At this time the Bowery was much changed, for one thing it was much smaller, for another it was fortressed by tall luxurious towers.

There were still a few who could challenge thirty thirsty camels and could skirt around the wealth to gain entrance to the few remaining flop houses located there but most could not. Those who could not took to the streets and made their nests at the crack between the sidewalk and the façade.

Bums were not called bums at this time, they were called alcoholics or addicts. Some sought refuge in Alcoholic Anonymous and in many of its offshoots, but most just up and died. No that is not quite right, they never got up, they just died.

While Billy was in one of those "give your full attention to your breathing states," it happened that for about one minute, Billy's time with glorious speed surged forward and his sense of strength expanded with splendid force.

Billy experienced for the first time what if felt like to be a man.

Through all the joy, one second took the time to contrast how Billy felt now as a man, to how he felt during his entire life.

The contrast did show that he lived his` life with his time suspended and the emotional fears of a ten year old child.

It seems ironic that Billy was stuck in his childhood precisely because he did not have one.

Billy was too young to know that being loyal to a father's illness is not the same as being loyal to a father.

Look carefully, it can happen.

Now the choices!

I prefer *

With knowledge of real time, experiencing real strength and the journey completed:
Billy the man, did after all,

Live happily ever after.

I prefer **

Certain things in life just cannot be fixed, the damage too great, the wounds too deep, the blows too hard.

The feeling of being a man never did return. The journey to the present was only half the voyage. The other half was the journey back to childhood.

Nonetheless Billy was happy. For the fleeting moment that, though it did make his childlike state more painful, it did give him the opportunity to see how things could have been.

73

Let us hope that in the future the devastation will be seen quickly, the science act swiftly, and the Billys, Florries and Bills of the future will indeed;

Live Happily Ever After

74

I prefer my own ending ***

The author invites you to write
an ending to this tale that would
be more to your liking.

Good Luck

75

At this time

76

The Flight Ends

77

78

I just heard from my publisher that in order for my book to have a spine text, I have to have twenty more pages of text, so it seems the flight has to continue.

The spine text is necessary as I have applied for a copyright for this tale, Therefore a copy of it will rest in the hallowed halls of the National Library for many years to come, and if ever called for, I want this tale to appear with as much dignity as a proper book cover can afford.

Florrie was not the typical unwed mother, if you could believe her. She said that she was with William James Kerr to help mend the heartbreak she was feeling at the time because her true love, her would be future husband, Patrick Reilly, was not there with her.

She said that in her weakened condition she could not resist the blarney and the passions of an Irish twenty year old.

80

Paddy and Florrie, as well as most people who lived in the town of Manchester, Connecticut, worked in the Hilliard's Woolen Mill. Manchester with its cloth mills was a natural destination for those coming from Belfast, Ireland. That city also had cloth mills, linen mills. The work requirements in all cloth mills were the same, no matter what the fabric.

People thought Patrick Reilly was over six feet tall and he was. Every inch of him was real. He was a year older than his Florence. Back in the old country, in order to support his family he had to leave Queens University where he was studying philosophy and was a striker on their soccer team. After leaving school he worked in one of the linen mills of Belfast before he was recruited to work in the Hilliard's Woolen Mill.

With his mill experience, strong back and willing hands, he was much sought after.

82

Although his auburn hair, gemstone blue eyes and teeth as white as they had right to be made him in great demand with the ladies, his only interest was in wooing his beloved Florence. His ready smile, laughter and kindness were true as they had their origins in his heart.

83

84

It had been just a few months since Patrick's death.

Paddy fell into one of the Hilliard
Woolen Mill's vats of boiling dye.

There was no such thing as compensation in those days. If you were hurt or killed on the job it was assumed that you did something wrong. It was your misfortune, or better yet, it was the will of God.

I wonder what it was that Paddy did that warranted him to be boiled to death.

The truth of Florrie's story could be confirmed by the fact that for many many years, every time she visited Manchester she would disappear for a few hours to visit the grave of her longed for true love.

88

It is not known exactly when Florrie traveled alone to New York City and got a room in the Dodson Hotel located on First Avenue to wait for the first signs of labor. The Dodson Hotel's only attribute was that it was located very near Belleview Hospital.

In those days, that was the hospital where immigrant unwed women went to have their babies, alone, away from all family and friends. It was only after twenty four hours of agonizing labor and the use of the steel forceps that the girl child allowed herself to come into this world.

89

The forceps made a permanent indentation on the right side of her skull above her hairline.

The crying the baby did was not to fill her lungs with air but was to express the unhappiness she felt that it was only she and her lonely disgraced mother that were in Belleview Hospital's delivery room with its light green tiled walls.

90

Luckily, the child's scalp indention did not affect her brain. That was evidenced by the fact that she, when an adult, and her husband, who never talked about his survival of the Second World War's Battle of the Budge, pioneered via a Greyhound bus to Berkeley, California.

There, they attended and graduated from its university.

Then they pioneered onward via U-Haul to Palo Alto, California, where they got in involved in

land

91

and

92

became two of the first self-made double digit millionaires of that city before it became part of Silicon Valley bloom.

93

This daughter born in the room with the light green tile walls paid too much attention to the relationship between the overly concerned mother and the dependent son, completely ignoring and denying the devastating relationship between the cruel father and the dependent son. This allowed her to righteously with-hold any generosity whatsoever she might have normally bestowed on Billy. This daughter was generous as long you were not her brother or for that matter her sister.

She did though, in her early pre-California days help Billy get to his first psychiatrist, and introduced him to gymnastics and to skiing. Billy did love her for that.

At thirty five, Billy could do an iron cross on the rings and ski, in icy conditions, the double black diamond Upper Goat. This is the most difficult trail on Mt. Mansfield, Stowe, Vermont.

95

Her husband showed much kindness to Billy. Again it was one of those special relationships.
I guess it was that they were kindred spirits.
Both had their secrets to keep. Their secrets were of wars, one a public war the other a familial war. Billy was convinced that it was not the heart of this father of four that caused his early demise, but it was his keeping the secrets of that bloody combat.

TICK 96

William James Kerr married Florrie only after succumbing to pressures from her sisters. Florrie only wanted him to marry her so that her infant daughter would have a proper name. She proposed that they get married so their child's birth certificate would read true and then they could divorce. She wanted nothing more from him than that.

98

Years later Florrie would recount the story that when she reminded her husband about the their marriage agreement, he grabbed up the startled infant, swirled around and shouted that she was not going to make a whore out of his child.

It looks like in spite of his hatred of the Catholic Church, their no divorce teachings did have an effect on his life.

TICK 99

Seeing that the mayhem started when this daughter born in the hospital near the Dodson Hotel was older, sixteen to be exact, because she had the strength of a little man with a crew cut, was a street fighter, wise beyond her years and a self-protector, his first attempt resulted in his being locked out the next drunken Saturday night.

Since she wanted everything in her life to be beautiful, she was able to attribute her leaving Hunter College at sixteen to go to live with her Aunt Cissy who lived on Sigourney Street in Hartford Connecticut, very near the Aetna Insurance Company, to her sense of adventure.

Newly arrived in the insurance capital of the world, she worked for Aetna, got a boyfriend and everything was again perfect.

Little did she realize once the monster was released, he would soon strike again.

103

William James Kerr, an avid
reader himself, was one of only a
handful of people who voluntarily
read James Joyce's "Ulysses." He
was so completely self-involved
did he not know that his only son
although very bright did not know
how to read. This was just one of
many ways that Bill showed that
he did not care what happened to
his disliked son.

104

That is not entirely true, one day when Billy was about seventeen years old, Bill took him to an outlet, a store returned—men's suit outlet. The returned suits were draped over contoured hangers that hung from plain iron pipe racks. It seems that Bill learned that his devoted friend, whom he met in a bar two nights ago, was employed at that outlet as a salesman. Bill could not wait to take advantage of the real cheap prices.

105

He took Billy there. Billy picked out a nice blue serge suit and Bill in a great puff of show generosity, paid for it.

Bill did not look through the scores and scores of suits hanging there from the plain pipe racks for a suit for himself.

Bill bought his many suits from "Bonds", the Saks Fifth Avenue of the Bronx.

Years later, Bill asked Billy;
"Do you remember the time when
I bought you that suit?"
That one time buying of anything
for his only son, must have left an
indelible mark on Bill's miserly
brain.

Billy meekly nodded, "yes."
That one time buying of that suit
from a plain pipe rack warehouse
by his Bonds bedecked father left
lasting scar on Billy's "unworthy"
brain.

Bill's second daughter was the most beautiful of all the children of both extended families. Unfortunately her good looks did not protect her. It was her nose that set the stage for a very beautiful face, or maybe it was her infectious smile, or just the vitality and radiance of her youth, that made her the subject of so many boy dreams. She wore that coronet with modesty, which only added to the delight.

109

She to, had a secret.
She accepted the mantel of big sister with grace, but their secrets bound them in an isolation so distant it could be measured only in star distances.

TOCK 110

It was her in the middle of the night scream that ended the violence but could not and did not end the nightmares.

Bill's snow bird nest in Florida was a petite banana yellow trailer that had rust where the wheels should have been.

William James Kerr drove a Ford Cortina then. He did not have to pay extra for the faulty electric system, it came standard for all Ford Cortinas.

What he liked most about his winter digs was that it made living in Florida cheap.

His castle was located near the Hollywood Municipal Golf Course. He played there because it was cheap.

112

On the morning of March 17th 1971, Bill made a birdie on the ninth hole, putting him on par for the course. The time was exactly10:23 am.

That is known because in addition to recording his score on the score card, he recorded the time.

Immediately after that he experienced a slight tightness in his chest. Because he did not have a "go to" friend, he had to drive himself to the hospital.

The nearest hospital was Saint Augustina of Hippo.

113

Despite his long held beliefs, he allowed himself to be admitted to this faith based medical center.
He was treated by three doctors. The first an emergency room doctor, the second a staff doctor and third a supervising doctor, The three were not too concerned because after examining him and conversing with him for quite some time, they concurred the man had just suffered a slight, mild myocardial infraction.

114

As sometimes happens to people with his condition, Bill became emboldened. That along with his magnifying unease with his surroundings compelled him to ask the questions that he hoped would reveal that at least one of these well-educated and well-off men would express some doubt. But to his increasing worry, all three doctors were believers in Christ.

He must have been well liked at the city run golf club because after learning that he died that day, the members decided to establish a tournament in his name.

I do not think it lasted more than a year, but the important thing is that they thought enough of him to establish the tournament in the first place.

His family was never a part of this honor, or for that matter never part of anything to do with William James Kerr's private life.

William James Kerr was certainly one of M. Scott Peck's "People of the Lie."

He left this planet with his still good looks intact. His one and only regret was, that the timing of the tightness did not allow him to boast to his new devoted friends about his making "par for the course" for the first time.

Florence Kerr, was of two minds when she was at the ceremony that ended when, "he" and his newest Bond suit, went up in flames.

She was not thinking about the man, the one who made her feel so unloved. She knew how she felt about him. She knew all that stinginess was not so much about the money as it was about the man.

But that occasion did cause her ponder about life, her life.

It was about a month after the blaze when one of her two conflicting thoughts or to be more accurate, moods, became dominant.

One evening when Billy went to their, now her, apartment that had a balcony, located at 3589 Fordham Road, that he became aware there was a stunning difference in his mother. He asked her what happened.

She answered, "She did not know, something just came over her."

Billy soon came to realize that the something was happiness, pure undiluted happiness. If ever happiness was manifest, it was that night.

A sense of gladness and wellbeing enveloped her. She was radiant.

Billy, although he himself continued to be ravaged, was happy to report that the feelings of joy, of cheerfulness, of contentment that she was experiencing stayed with his mother.

TOCK **120**

Those feelings were still there when in the late afternoon of Wednesday, May 23rd, 1972, Florrie flew away to be with her cherished Paddy.

121

Again, At this time

122

This Low Flying Flight Ends

Tick

Tock

CPSIA information can be obtained at www.ICGtesting.com
Printed in the USA
LVOW061401200712

290912LV00001B/17/P